序 言

　　本書自第一冊出版以來，深受各界好評，聽力測驗的訓練，愈多愈好。學生只有在參加模擬測驗的時候，才會專心，上聽力課，才不會睡覺。

　　英語能力分級檢定測驗依不同英語程度，分爲初、中、中高、高和優等五級，預計測驗時間爲兩個小時，一般民眾通過中級英語能力檢定測驗之後，可以此做爲就業或申請學校的證明。教育部待這項測驗發展穩定後，結合大學入學考試，擴充認證制度功能。

　　第二冊書分爲八回，每回考試時間爲 40 分鐘，每回測驗分爲四部份，和教育部的中級英語檢定測驗相同。這八回測驗，每回都經過劉毅英文聽力班實際考試，以每題 1.67 分計算，最高分介於 79 分至 86 分之間，最低分介於 35 至 42 分之間。每份考題能考 60 分以上，算及格。本試題比實際考試稍微深一點，特別是第四部份，如此才能從此資料中，聽力獲得增進。

　　本書是依據「英語能力分級檢定」測驗指標，在單字爲五千字的範圍內，可聽懂對話及廣播。要在聽力一項得高分，就是要不斷練習，現在在校的高中學生，早晚都要參加此項考試，要及早準備，爲學校爭光。本書另附有教師手冊。

編者 謹識

本書製作過程

Test Book No. 9, 12, 15 由謝靜芳老師負責, Test Book No. 10, 13, 16 由蔡琇瑩老師負責,No. 11, 14 由高瑋謙老師負責。每份試題均由三位老師,在聽力班實際測驗過,經過每週一次測驗後,立刻講解的方式,學生們的聽力有明顯的進步,在大學甄試聽力考試中,都輕鬆過關。三位老師們的共同看法是,要在聽力方面得高分,就要不斷練習,愈多愈好。聽力訓練,愈早開始愈好。

本書另附有教師手冊,附有答案及詳解,售價 180 元。
錄音帶八卷,售價 960 元。

English Listening Comprehension Test

Test Book No. 9

This listening comprehension test will test your ability to understand spoken English. In this test, each conversation, statement and question will be spoken JUST ONE TIME. They will not be written out for you. There are four parts to this test. Special instructions will be given to you at the beginning of each part.

Part A

In Part A, you will see several pictures in your test book. For each picture, you will be asked 1 to 3 questions. For each question, you will hear four possible answers. Choose the best answer according to what you see in the picture.

Example:

You will see:

You will hear: What is this?
　　　　　　　　A. This is a table.
　　　　　　　　B. This is a chair.
　　　　　　　　C. This is a watch.
　　　　　　　　D. This is a doll.

The best answer to the question "What is this?" is B: "This is a chair."   Therefore, you should choose answer B.

A. <u>Questions 1-3</u>

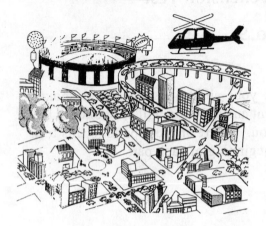

D. <u>Questions 8-9</u>

B. <u>Question 4</u>

E. <u>Questions 10-12</u>

C. <u>Questions 5-7</u>

F. <u>Questions 13-15</u>

Part B

In Part B, you will hear 15 questions.　After you hear a question, read the four possible answers in your test book and decide which one is the best answer to the question you have heard.

Example:

　You will hear:　What does your father do?

　You will read:　A. He's 50 years old.
　　　　　　　　　B. He's a teacher.
　　　　　　　　　C. He's hungry.
　　　　　　　　　D. He's in Los Angeles.

The best answer to the question "What does your father do?" is B: "He's a teacher." Therefore, you should choose answer B.

Please go to the next page. ⇨

16. A. I am so surprised.
    B. Of course, you got it.
    C. Yes, I mean it.
    D. You have to study hard.

17. A. My friends are.
    B. They are singing.
    C. There is one boy in the classroom.
    D. They are my classmates.

18. A. It's too little to spend.
    B. A deal is a deal.
    C. Will that be cash?
    D. Thank you very much.

19. A. May I help you?
    B. Can I do you a favor?
    C. What size of Coke, sir?
    D. What would you like?

20. A. By car.
    B. Once a week.
    C. Two times.
    D. Eight hours a day.

21. A. Cheer up!
    B. That's all right.
    C. Thank you.
    D. You are very kind.

22. A. They had a good time.
    B. For an hour.
    C. About two weeks.
    D. At three o'clock.

23. A. What did you lose?
    B. We'll lose a lot of money.
    C. Don't worry. We can ask the boy over there.
    D. I don't know how much we lost.

24. A. Yes, it's their house.
    B. Yes, they are.
    C. No, they are our house.
    D. No, it's their house.

25. A. My chair is broken.
    B. My watch was lost.
    C. I have good luck.
    D. Yes, no problem.

26. A. Yes, there are any birds in it.
    B. No, there are not some.
    C. Yes, there are some.
    D. Yes, there is some.

27. A. Am I?
    B. You did?
    C. Thank you.
    D. Oh, my goodness.

28. A. How do you know it?
    B. Of course, they are not enough.
    C. Sure, more than enough.
    D. Who are you talking about?

29. A. That's all right.
    B. I'll come here again.
    C. I got up late.
    D. I am so surprised.

30. A. Sometimes I go by bus, and sometimes by bicycle.
    B. The bus is faster; bicycles are too slow.
    C. I never ride my bicycle to work.
    D. I sometimes work on Sunday.

Part C

In Part C, you will hear 15 conversations between a man and a woman. After each conversation, you will hear a question about the conversation. After you hear the question, read the four possible answers in your test book and choose the best answer to the question you have heard.

Example:

<u>You will hear:</u> (Man) How do you go to school every day?
(Woman) Usually by bus. Sometimes by taxi.

TONE: How does the woman go to school?

<u>You will read:</u> A. She always goes to school on foot.
B. She usually takes a bike.
C. She takes either a bus or a taxi.
D. She usually goes to school by bus, never by taxi.

The best answer to the question "How does the woman go to school?" is C: "She takes either a bus or a taxi." Therefore, you should choose answer C.

Please go to the next page. ⇨

31. A. Finish checking his references.
    B. Complete the research.
    C. Put the material in order.
    D. Finish typing the paper.

32. A. Go to the lab briefly.
    B. Check on what's for dinner.
    C. Go running before they eat.
    D. See if they have plenty of work.

33. A. Write.
    B. Study.
    C. Shop.
    D. Eat.

34. A. He doesn't keep his promises.
    B. He's very trustworthy.
    C. He's not really busy.
    D. Phil will help.

35. A. The tickets were sold out.
    B. The play was called off.
    C. The play wasn't interesting.
    D. The weather was too cold.

36. A. In a library.
    B. In a bookstore.
    C. In a post office.
    D. In a supermarket.

37. A. He fell.
    B. He had a fight.
    C. He was killed.
    D. He was punished.

38. A. Writing checks for tickets.
    B. A train trip.
    C. Today's rainstorm.
    D. Using their tickets.

39. A. If he'll have time to eat in Chicago
    B. Where the bus station is located.
    C. When buses depart for Chicago.
    D. If he can catch a bus that leaves Chicago.

40. A. A garage.
    B. An airport.
    C. A dentist's office.
    D. A construction company.

41. A. In a spacecraft.
    B. On the moon.
    C. In an observatory.
    D. In an astronomy class.

42. A. It might rain.
    B. She's afraid of open windows on trains.
    C. Her suitcase is too full to close.
    D. The drains are clogged up.

43. A. Pick things up.
    B. Wash the floor.
    C. Write a book.
    D. Lie down.

44. A. It's filled with lies.
    B. It doesn't describe all her experience.
    C. It is too long.
    D. It contains one lie.

45. A. He should run more.
    B. He asks too many questions.
    C. He wants to be president.
    D. He has a good imagination.

Part D

In Part D, you will hear 15 short talks.   After each talk, you will hear a question about the talk.   After you hear the question, read the four possible answers in your test book and choose the best answer to the question you have heard.

Example:

You will hear: Well, that's all for Unit 15.   For today's homework, please do the review questions on page 80, and we'll check the answers tomorrow. Now, let's go on to Unit 16.

TONE: What is the teacher going to do next in today's class?

You will read: A. Check the homework.
B. Review Unit 15.
C. Start a new unit.
D. Answer students' questions.

The best answer to the question "What is the teacher going to do next in today's class?" is C: "Start a new unit."   Therefore, you should choose answer C.

Please go to the next page. ⇨

46. A. The giant bird cage.
    B. The tiger house.
    C. The monkey and ape habitat.
    D. The tropical rainforest exhibit.

47. A. From affluent merchants.
    B. From his father.
    C. From classes at school.
    D. From his co-workers.

48. A. A dance club.
    B. A student arts committee.
    C. A group of professors.
    D. A sports team.

49. A. It would be too long.
    B. It would be more difficult to read.
    C. It could not be copied easily.
    D. It could not be handed in on time.

50. A. A telephone.
    B. A person.
    C. A communication system.
    D. A television.

51. A. Cutting a field.
    B. Talking with newsmen.
    C. Jogging.
    D. Fishing.

52. A. 98.6.
    B. 37.
    C. Body temperature.
    D. A temperature scale.

53. A. A frying pan.
    B. An omelet.
    C. A telephone.
    D. A fair.

54. A. At a store.
    B. At a warehouse.
    C. In a video arcade.
    D. In a school.

55. A. 10 points.
    B. 2 points.
    C. 15 points.
    D. 5 points.

56. A. Radios.
    B. Coins for telephones.
    C. Palmtop computers.
    D. Ordinary beepers.

57. A. A doctor.
    B. A circus act.
    C. A bilingual aide.
    D. A clown.

58. A. The home team won.
    B. It ended in a tie.
    C. The crowd ruined the game.
    D. The Rams won.

59. A. A concert pianist.
    B. A builder.
    C. A jazz musician.
    D. An astronaut.

60. A. At a concert.
    B. At a sports event.
    C. At a bank.
    D. At a stage play.

中級英語聽力檢定測驗答案紙

中文姓名 _____　　測驗日期：民國 ____ 年 ____ 月 ____ 日

1. 准考證號碼	2. 出　　生			3. 國民身分證統一編號
	年(民國)	月	日	

請依序將每個數字在下欄塗黑

＊注意：本答案紙限用 #2 (HB) 黑色
　　　　鉛筆在「○」內塗黑、塗滿。

作答樣例：　正　確　　　錯　誤

聽　力　測　驗			
試題別			
試題冊號碼			

1 Ⓐ Ⓑ Ⓒ Ⓓ　　11 Ⓐ Ⓑ Ⓒ Ⓓ　　21 Ⓐ Ⓑ Ⓒ Ⓓ　　31 Ⓐ Ⓑ Ⓒ Ⓓ　　41 Ⓐ Ⓑ Ⓒ Ⓓ　　51 Ⓐ Ⓑ Ⓒ Ⓓ

2 Ⓐ Ⓑ Ⓒ Ⓓ　　12 Ⓐ Ⓑ Ⓒ Ⓓ　　22 Ⓐ Ⓑ Ⓒ Ⓓ　　32 Ⓐ Ⓑ Ⓒ Ⓓ　　42 Ⓐ Ⓑ Ⓒ Ⓓ　　52 Ⓐ Ⓑ Ⓒ Ⓓ

3 Ⓐ Ⓑ Ⓒ Ⓓ　　13 Ⓐ Ⓑ Ⓒ Ⓓ　　23 Ⓐ Ⓑ Ⓒ Ⓓ　　33 Ⓐ Ⓑ Ⓒ Ⓓ　　43 Ⓐ Ⓑ Ⓒ Ⓓ　　53 Ⓐ Ⓑ Ⓒ Ⓓ

4 Ⓐ Ⓑ Ⓒ Ⓓ　　14 Ⓐ Ⓑ Ⓒ Ⓓ　　24 Ⓐ Ⓑ Ⓒ Ⓓ　　34 Ⓐ Ⓑ Ⓒ Ⓓ　　44 Ⓐ Ⓑ Ⓒ Ⓓ　　54 Ⓐ Ⓑ Ⓒ Ⓓ

5 Ⓐ Ⓑ Ⓒ Ⓓ　　15 Ⓐ Ⓑ Ⓒ Ⓓ　　25 Ⓐ Ⓑ Ⓒ Ⓓ　　35 Ⓐ Ⓑ Ⓒ Ⓓ　　45 Ⓐ Ⓑ Ⓒ Ⓓ　　55 Ⓐ Ⓑ Ⓒ Ⓓ

6 Ⓐ Ⓑ Ⓒ Ⓓ　　16 Ⓐ Ⓑ Ⓒ Ⓓ　　26 Ⓐ Ⓑ Ⓒ Ⓓ　　36 Ⓐ Ⓑ Ⓒ Ⓓ　　46 Ⓐ Ⓑ Ⓒ Ⓓ　　56 Ⓐ Ⓑ Ⓒ Ⓓ

7 Ⓐ Ⓑ Ⓒ Ⓓ　　17 Ⓐ Ⓑ Ⓒ Ⓓ　　27 Ⓐ Ⓑ Ⓒ Ⓓ　　37 Ⓐ Ⓑ Ⓒ Ⓓ　　47 Ⓐ Ⓑ Ⓒ Ⓓ　　57 Ⓐ Ⓑ Ⓒ Ⓓ

8 Ⓐ Ⓑ Ⓒ Ⓓ　　18 Ⓐ Ⓑ Ⓒ Ⓓ　　28 Ⓐ Ⓑ Ⓒ Ⓓ　　38 Ⓐ Ⓑ Ⓒ Ⓓ　　48 Ⓐ Ⓑ Ⓒ Ⓓ　　58 Ⓐ Ⓑ Ⓒ Ⓓ

9 Ⓐ Ⓑ Ⓒ Ⓓ　　19 Ⓐ Ⓑ Ⓒ Ⓓ　　29 Ⓐ Ⓑ Ⓒ Ⓓ　　39 Ⓐ Ⓑ Ⓒ Ⓓ　　49 Ⓐ Ⓑ Ⓒ Ⓓ　　59 Ⓐ Ⓑ Ⓒ Ⓓ

10 Ⓐ Ⓑ Ⓒ Ⓓ　　20 Ⓐ Ⓑ Ⓒ Ⓓ　　30 Ⓐ Ⓑ Ⓒ Ⓓ　　40 Ⓐ Ⓑ Ⓒ Ⓓ　　50 Ⓐ Ⓑ Ⓒ Ⓓ　　60 Ⓐ Ⓑ Ⓒ Ⓓ

English Listening Comprehension Test

Test Book No. 10

This listening comprehension test will test your ability to understand spoken English. In this test, each conversation, statement and question will be spoken JUST ONE TIME. They will not be written out for you. There are four parts to this test. Special instructions will be given to you at the beginning of each part.

Part A

In Part A, you will see several pictures in your test book. For each picture, you will be asked 1 to 3 questions. For each question, you will hear four possible answers. Choose the best answer according to what you see in the picture.

Example:

You will see:

You will hear: What is this?
A. This is a table.
B. This is a chair.
C. This is a watch.
D. This is a doll.

The best answer to the question "What is this?" is B: "This is a chair." Therefore, you should choose answer B.

A. Questions 1-3

B. Questions 4-6

C. Questions 7-9

D. Questions 10-12

E. Questions 13-15

Part B

In Part B, you will hear 15 questions.   After you hear a question, read the four possible answers in your test book and decide which one is the best answer to the question you have heard.

Example:

<u>You will hear:</u>   What does your father do?

<u>You will read:</u>   A. He's 50 years old.
                    B. He's a teacher.
                    C. He's hungry.
                    D. He's in Los Angeles.

The best answer to the question "What does your father do?" is B: "He's a teacher." Therefore, you should choose answer B.

Please go to the next page. ⇨

16. A. I am afraid I can't.
    B. No, we'd love to.
    C. We're going to.
    D. I am afraid so.

17. A. I am sorry to do so.
    B. No, thanks.
    C. I'd be happy to help.
    D. Yes, thank you.

18. A. They are all six for five cents.
    B. Yes, they are cheap.
    C. All right. I'll buy six.
    D. It costs fifty cents.

19. A. That's a good idea.
    B. Yes, thanks.
    C. Yes, tea is cheaper.
    D. Coffee, please.

20. A. Are you?
    B. Where, where.
    C. Thank you.
    D. You are right.

21. A. Let me to see it.
    B. Really? Have you got a computer?
    C. When did you bought it?
    D. How much you cost it?

22. A. I like vacation very much.
    B. I have no idea.
    C. It always comes in February.
    D. Everything is all right.

23. A. That's all right.
    B. Well, you can go.
    C. Why must we go?
    D. It sounds great.

24. A. Forty years old.
    B. He's fine, thank you.
    C. He's old.
    D. A bus driver.

25. A. At nine-forty.
    B. In the evening.
    C. I usually go to bed at ten.
    D. I sometimes go to bed late.

26. A. My brother does.
    B. My sister will.
    C. My mother did.
    D. My father has.

27. A. No, he isn't.
    B. No, I think not.
    C. No, I don't think it.
    D. No, I think so.

28. A. He gets up every morning.
    B. He usually goes to school at 7:00.
    C. He gets up early.
    D. He usually gets up at 6:30.

29. A. Yes, I do. I do have two sisters.
    B. No, I don't. I have only two brothers.
    C. No, she doesn't. She has two sisters.
    D. Yes, she does. She has two sisters.

30. A. Because we have to study on Monday.
    B. We have a lot of free time on that day.
    C. It will rain on Monday.
    D. Some friends came to visit me on Monday.

Part C

In Part C, you will hear 15 conversations between a man and a woman. After each conversation, you will hear a question about the conversation. After you hear the question, read the four possible answers in your test book and choose the best answer to the question you have heard.

Example:

You will hear: (Man)   How do you go to school every day?
                 (Woman)   Usually by bus. Sometimes by taxi.

                 TONE: How does the woman go to school?

You will read: A. She always goes to school on foot.
                 B. She usually takes a bike.
                 C. She takes either a bus or a taxi.
                 D. She usually goes to school by bus, never by taxi.

The best answer to the question "How does the woman go to school?" is C: "She takes either a bus or a taxi." Therefore, you should choose answer C.

Please go to the next page. ⇨

31. A. To mail a letter and a check.
    B. To buy stamps.
    C. To get a package.
    D. To draw a check to the postman.

32. A. Use prepared cake mixes.
    B. Cut another piece of cake.
    C. Start baking from scratch.
    D. Buy a moist cake.

33. A. He works three times as much as he did before.
    B. He has two free days for every three days he works.
    C. He works three nights every two weeks.
    D. He has twice as much work as he used to have.

34. A. He will get angry.
    B. He is looking for a parking space.
    C. He has to buy a parking ticket.
    D. He will discover it himself.

35. A. Only if it is always in sight.
    B. No, because she asked him to turn it off between problems.
    C. He should leave it on the table.
    D. No, because he asked for it.

36. A. Because you must take the stairs.
    B. Because nine is an odd number.
    C. Because the elevator got stuck.
    D. Because there are too many people in the elevator.

37. A. Because it is customary.
    B. Because he had extra money.
    C. Because the lady lost her money by mistake.
    D. Because the musician took a shower.

38. A. The vacation has been too long.
    B. The lady smells musty.
    C. The lady smells something musty.
    D. The windows are open.

39. A. 7:10
    B. 7:00
    C. 6:50
    D. 7:05

40. A. The brothers have moved away.
    B. It is not his affair.
    C. The brothers don't know.
    D. He doesn't know the way.

41. A. In an electrical shop.
    B. At a college.
    C. In an airport.
    D. At a voting booth.

42. A. A field trip.
    B. A hut in the woods.
    C. A bad dream.
    D. A footrace.

43. A. She is pitiful.
    B. She is too shy to apply.
    C. They are afraid of her.
    D. She is intelligent.

44. A. They haven't seen any.
    B. They have seen enough.
    C. They can't afford one.
    D. They have an apartment.

45. A. She feels bad.
    B. She hasn't been to dinner.
    C. Her boyfriend has been at her house all day.
    D. Jane is having dinner.

Part D

In Part D, you will hear 15 short talks.   After each talk, you will hear a question about the talk.   After you hear the question, read the four possible answers in your test book and choose the best answer to the question you have heard.

Example:

You will hear: Well, that's all for Unit 15.   For today's homework, please do the review questions on page 80, and we'll check the answers tomorrow. Now, let's go on to Unit 16.

TONE: What is the teacher going to do next in today's class?

You will read: A. Check the homework.
　　　　　　　 B. Review Unit 15.
　　　　　　　 C. Start a new unit.
　　　　　　　 D. Answer students' questions.

The best answer to the question "What is the teacher going to do next in today's class?" is C: "Start a new unit."   Therefore, you should choose answer C.

Please go to the next page. ⇨

46. A. She took art lessons.
    B. She went to lots of museums.
    C. She went swimming with her friends.
    D. She took swimming lessons.

47. A. A president.
    B. A filmmaker.
    C. An author.
    D. An actor.

48. A. She doesn't teach mathematics.
    B. She has a good sense of humor.
    C. She likes George very much.
    D. She has many friends.

49. A. In high school.
    B. When he entered college.
    C. After his second year of high school.
    D. After his second year of college.

50. A. She takes care of the layout.
    B. She's the general editor.
    C. She's in charge of the fiction page.
    D. She edits the cooking page.

51. A. A market research company.
    B. A news agency.
    C. A dating agency.
    D. A private detective agency.

52. A. The toy department.
    B. The pet department.
    C. The women's jeans department.
    D. The women's sportswear department.

53. A. Information about immigration.
    B. A visa.
    C. A landing card.
    D. Duty-free goods.

54. A. It's going to cease to exist in some areas.
    B. It's going to improve on the whole.
    C. It's going to be flooded with competition.
    D. It's going to develop in Florida.

55. A. Cathy's family visited Mami.
    B. Cathy came to see Mami from Scotland.
    C. Mami enjoyed her holiday in Switzerland.
    D. Mami had a good time in Scotland.

56. A. Thursday, June 2.
    B. Saturday, June 4.
    C. Thursday, June 23.
    D. Saturday, June 25.

57. A. An optometrist.
    B. A professor.
    C. A pharmacist.
    D. A dentist.

58. A. Tower A and B.
    B. Tower C.
    C. Tower D.
    D. Tower E.

59. A. As a liquid medicine.
    B. As a drink in ceremonies.
    C. As a health drink mixed with sugar.
    D. As a popular drink.

60. A. About 6%.
    B. About 16%.
    C. About 60%.
    D. About 66%.

中級英語聽力檢定測驗答案紙

中文姓名 _____　　測驗日期：民國 _____ 年 _____ 月 _____ 日

1. 准考證號碼					2. 出　　　生						3. 國民身分證統一編號									
					年(民國)		月		日											
請依序將每個數字在下欄塗黑																				

＊注意：本答案紙限用 #2 (HB) 黑色
鉛筆在「○」內塗黑、塗滿。

作答樣例：　正　確　　　錯　誤

聽　力　測　驗				
試題別				
試題冊號碼				

1 ⒶⒷⒸⒹ　　11 ⒶⒷⒸⒹ　　21 ⒶⒷⒸⒹ　　31 ⒶⒷⒸⒹ　　41 ⒶⒷⒸⒹ　　51 ⒶⒷⒸⒹ

2 ⒶⒷⒸⒹ　　12 ⒶⒷⒸⒹ　　22 ⒶⒷⒸⒹ　　32 ⒶⒷⒸⒹ　　42 ⒶⒷⒸⒹ　　52 ⒶⒷⒸⒹ

3 ⒶⒷⒸⒹ　　13 ⒶⒷⒸⒹ　　23 ⒶⒷⒸⒹ　　33 ⒶⒷⒸⒹ　　43 ⒶⒷⒸⒹ　　53 ⒶⒷⒸⒹ

4 ⒶⒷⒸⒹ　　14 ⒶⒷⒸⒹ　　24 ⒶⒷⒸⒹ　　34 ⒶⒷⒸⒹ　　44 ⒶⒷⒸⒹ　　54 ⒶⒷⒸⒹ

5 ⒶⒷⒸⒹ　　15 ⒶⒷⒸⒹ　　25 ⒶⒷⒸⒹ　　35 ⒶⒷⒸⒹ　　45 ⒶⒷⒸⒹ　　55 ⒶⒷⒸⒹ

6 ⒶⒷⒸⒹ　　16 ⒶⒷⒸⒹ　　26 ⒶⒷⒸⒹ　　36 ⒶⒷⒸⒹ　　46 ⒶⒷⒸⒹ　　56 ⒶⒷⒸⒹ

7 ⒶⒷⒸⒹ　　17 ⒶⒷⒸⒹ　　27 ⒶⒷⒸⒹ　　37 ⒶⒷⒸⒹ　　47 ⒶⒷⒸⒹ　　57 ⒶⒷⒸⒹ

8 ⒶⒷⒸⒹ　　18 ⒶⒷⒸⒹ　　28 ⒶⒷⒸⒹ　　38 ⒶⒷⒸⒹ　　48 ⒶⒷⒸⒹ　　58 ⒶⒷⒸⒹ

9 ⒶⒷⒸⒹ　　19 ⒶⒷⒸⒹ　　29 ⒶⒷⒸⒹ　　39 ⒶⒷⒸⒹ　　49 ⒶⒷⒸⒹ　　59 ⒶⒷⒸⒹ

10 ⒶⒷⒸⒹ　　20 ⒶⒷⒸⒹ　　30 ⒶⒷⒸⒹ　　40 ⒶⒷⒸⒹ　　50 ⒶⒷⒸⒹ　　60 ⒶⒷⒸⒹ

English Listening Comprehension Test

Test Book No. 11

This listening comprehension test will test your ability to understand spoken English.   In this test, each conversation, statement and question will be spoken JUST ONE TIME.   They will not be written out for you.   There are four parts to this test. Special instructions will be given to you at the beginning of each part.

Part A

In Part A, you will see several pictures in your test book.   For each picture, you will be asked 1 to 3 questions.   For each question, you will hear four possible answers. Choose the best answer according to what you see in the picture.

Example:

You will see:

You will hear:　　What is this?
　　　　　　　　　A. This is a table.
　　　　　　　　　B. This is a chair.
　　　　　　　　　C. This is a watch.
　　　　　　　　　D. This is a doll.

The best answer to the question "What is this?" is B: "This is a chair."   Therefore, you should choose answer B.

A. <u>Questions 1-2</u>

D. <u>Questions 9-10</u>

B. <u>Questions 3-6</u>

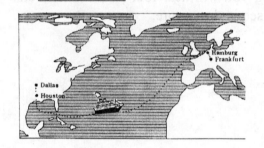

E. <u>Questions 11-13</u>

C. <u>Questions 7-8</u>

F. <u>Questions 14-15</u>

Part B

In Part B, you will hear 15 questions.　After you hear a question, read the four possible answers in your test book and decide which one is the best answer to the question you have heard.

Example:

You will hear:　What does your father do?

You will read:　A.　He's 50 years old.
　　　　　　　　B.　He's a teacher.
　　　　　　　　C.　He's hungry.
　　　　　　　　D.　He's in Los Angeles.

The best answer to the question "What does your father do?" is B: "He's a teacher." Therefore, you should choose answer B.

Please go to the next page. ⇨

16. A. It doesn't matter.
    B. It's a serious matter.
    C. It's out of order.
    D. I don't like the matter.

17. A. Thank you very much.
    B. I'm so surprised!
    C. All right!
    D. She had a cold.

18. A. Thank you very much.
    B. Sure, I'll take it.
    C. Everything is on sale today.
    D. Not so good.

19. A. In junior high school.
    B. Three years.
    C. Yes, I have.
    D. Almost every day.

20. A. He's not there.
    B. He's working in his office.
    C. I thought he went fishing.
    D. I asked him to wait.

21. A. It leaves at 10:30.
    B. It is 10:30 now.
    C. It is very early.
    D. It is getting a little late.

22. A. I don't like to play cards.
    B. No, when were you there?
    C. Did you lend me a deck of cards?
    D. No cake for me, thanks.

23. A. I am ready.
    B. I have lost my watch.
    C. I am not wrong.
    D. I have finished my work.

24. A. No, I don't like them.
    B. Yes, they are delicious.
    C. I would like some tea.
    D. That costs a lot of money.

25. A. By train.
    B. About ten days.
    C. In one week.
    D. Five hours ago.

26. A. Today is our first day of business.
    B. No, I'll just look around.
    C. Anything you want.
    D. Here you are!

27. A. So can I.
    B. It is summer, you know.
    C. I left my jacket in your room.
    D. You caught a cold.

28. A. Why not tell the police officers?
    B. I have a new one.
    C. Would you lend me yours?
    D. I am so excited.

29. A. It's over there.
    B. He called me an hour ago.
    C. That was my friend, Tom.
    D. This is Allen speaking.

30. A. Neither.   She is a nurse.
    B. Yes, she is.
    C. No, she isn't.
    D. Either one will do.

Part C

In Part C, you will hear 15 conversations between a man and a woman. After each conversation, you will hear a question about the conversation. After you hear the question, read the four possible answers in your test book and choose the best answer to the question you have heard.

Example:

You will hear: (Man)   How do you go to school every day?
                (Woman)   Usually by bus.   Sometimes by taxi.

                TONE: How does the woman go to school?

You will read: A. She always goes to school on foot.
                 B. She usually takes a bike.
                 C. She takes either a bus or a taxi.
                 D. She usually goes to school by bus, never by taxi.

The best answer to the question "How does the woman go to school?" is C: "She takes either a bus or a taxi."   Therefore, you should choose answer C.

Please go to the next page. ⇨

31. A. Political science.
    B. Economics.
    C. Getting an A.
    D. Political science and economics.

32. A. Changed her professor.
    B. Seen the professor.
    C. Changed her mind.
    D. Left school.

33. A. Her suitcase.
    B. Some rocks.
    C. The leaves.
    D. A down pillow.

34. A. Check the time of high tide.
    B. Go stand under the clock.
    C. Wait a little longer.
    D. Look for the traffic light.

35. A. Catch a cold.
    B. Hurry to catch the bus.
    C. Sit next to the bus stop.
    D. Fix his torn sleeve.

36. A. The room is on fire.
    B. They are bothered by the smoke.
    C. There is very little breeze.
    D. The men are not permitted in the room.

37. A. At a mine.
    B. In a new car showroom.
    C. In a parking lot.
    D. At a car repair shop.

38. A. They are both very tired of it.
    B. They are happy she's playing it at last.
    C. It is one of their favorite songs.
    D. They could listen to it another thousand times.

39. A. He's a boat builder.
    B. He smokes a pipe.
    C. He paints watercolors.
    D. He's a plumber.

40. A. A trip she has already taken.
    B. A trip she takes frequently.
    C. A restaurant she owns.
    D. A famous statue in Philadelphia.

41. A. Buying a new typewriter.
    B. Finding a new place for the typewriter.
    C. Finding a better typist.
    D. Questioning the typist.

42. A. Barry no longer lives in New York.
    B. Barry doesn't know how to economize.
    C. The woman called Barry in California.
    D. The woman didn't ever meet Barry.

43. A. Whether they should move west.
    B. A historical novel.
    C. Whether they once lived in the same town.
    D. A science course.

44. A. The ground is too hard for planting.
    B. Transportation is expensive from California.
    C. There has been too much rain in California.
    D. The planters are experimenting with new crops.

45. A. She was understanding.
    B. She was apologetic.
    C. She was annoyed.
    D. She was careless.

Part D

In Part D, you will hear 15 short talks.　After each talk, you will hear a question about the talk.　After you hear the question, read the four possible answers in your test book and choose the best answer to the question you have heard.

Example:

<u>You will hear</u>:　Well, that's all for Unit 15.　For today's homework, please do the review questions on page 80, and we'll check the answers tomorrow. Now, let's go on to Unit 16.

　　　　　　　　　　TONE:　What is the teacher going to do next in today's class?

<u>You will read</u>:　A.　Check the homework.
　　　　　　　　　　B.　Review Unit 15.
　　　　　　　　　　C.　Start a new unit.
　　　　　　　　　　D.　Answer students' questions.

The best answer to the question "What is the teacher going to do next in today's class?" is C: "Start a new unit."　Therefore, you should choose answer C.

Please go to the next page. ⇨

46. A. He has a part-time job.
    B. He goes to the park with his friends.
    C. He picks up his mother after work.
    D. He takes care of his sister.

47. A. Japan.
    B. Falling down a lot.
    C. For the first time in his life.
    D. Enjoying his time in the lodge.

48. A. The weather, museums, and parks are nice.
    B. The cable cars stop at all the museums.
    C. It's always filled with visitors.
    D. All the big parks have museums.

49. A. Hawaii.
    B. Okinawa.
    C. Both Hawaii and Okinawa.
    D. Neither Hawaii nor Okinawa.

50. A. In a public hall.
    B. In a science museum.
    C. In an examination hall.
    D. In a university lecture hall.

51. A. People with digestion problems.
    B. People with eating disorders.
    C. People who want to try a new, effective diet.
    D. People who have made themselves sick on various diets.

52. A. The adoption of a single global monetary unit.
    B. Economic superpower status.
    C. The installation of further trade barriers.
    D. The exclusion of all other countries from its trading system.

53. A. The teaching of "shop" skills to only boys.
    B. The teaching of home economics to only girls.
    C. The teaching of "shop" skills to only girls.
    D. The teaching of home economics to both sexes.

54. A. 6:30 a.m.
    B. 6:45 a.m.
    C. 11:30 a.m.
    D. 2:30 p.m.

55. A. Just after taking off in Miami.
    B. Just above the airport in Atlanta.
    C. Just after taking off in Jacksonville.
    D. Just above the St. Johns River.

56. A. In producing waste.
    B. In burning trash.
    C. In gaining weight.
    D. In driving cars.

57. A. A news item.
    B. An advertisement.
    C. A lecture.
    D. A tour description.

58. A. Someone was jealous of her.
    B. She was jealous of the murderer.
    C. She was a murderer.
    D. She committed suicide.

59. A. She killed them.
    B. She fed them.
    C. She rejected them.
    D. She rescued them.

60. A. It's about one-third.
    B. It's about half.
    C. It's about two-thirds.
    D. It's about the same.

中級英語聽力檢定測驗答案紙

中文姓名 _____　　測驗日期：民國 _____ 年 _____ 月 _____ 日

1. 准考證號碼	2. 出　　　生			3. 國民身分證統一編號
	年(民國)	月	日	

請依序將每個數字在下欄塗黑

准考證號碼欄：⓪①②③④⑤⑥⑦⑧⑨（五欄）

出生年(民國)：⓪①②③④⑤⑥⑦⑧⑨（兩欄）

月：①②③

日：⓪①②③④⑤⑥⑦⑧⑨（兩欄）

國民身分證統一編號欄字母：Ⓐ Ⓑ Ⓒ Ⓓ Ⓔ Ⓕ Ⓖ Ⓗ Ⓘ Ⓙ Ⓚ Ⓛ Ⓜ Ⓝ Ⓞ Ⓟ Ⓠ Ⓡ Ⓢ Ⓣ Ⓤ Ⓥ Ⓦ Ⓧ Ⓨ Ⓩ

國民身分證統一編號數字欄：⓪①②③④⑤⑥⑦⑧⑨（九欄）

＊注意：本答案紙限用 #2 (HB) 黑色鉛筆在「○」內塗黑、塗滿。

作答樣例：　正　確　　　　錯　誤

正確：Ⓐ Ⓑ ● Ⓓ

錯誤：Ⓐ Ⓑ ✓Ⓒ Ⓓ　　Ⓐ Ⓑ ✗Ⓒ Ⓓ　　Ⓐ Ⓑ ◉ Ⓓ　　Ⓐ Ⓑ ◖ Ⓓ

聽　力　測　驗				
試題別				
試題冊號碼				

1 ⒶⒷⒸⒹ　11 ⒶⒷⒸⒹ　21 ⒶⒷⒸⒹ　31 ⒶⒷⒸⒹ　41 ⒶⒷⒸⒹ　51 ⒶⒷⒸⒹ

2 ⒶⒷⒸⒹ　12 ⒶⒷⒸⒹ　22 ⒶⒷⒸⒹ　32 ⒶⒷⒸⒹ　42 ⒶⒷⒸⒹ　52 ⒶⒷⒸⒹ

3 ⒶⒷⒸⒹ　13 ⒶⒷⒸⒹ　23 ⒶⒷⒸⒹ　33 ⒶⒷⒸⒹ　43 ⒶⒷⒸⒹ　53 ⒶⒷⒸⒹ

4 ⒶⒷⒸⒹ　14 ⒶⒷⒸⒹ　24 ⒶⒷⒸⒹ　34 ⒶⒷⒸⒹ　44 ⒶⒷⒸⒹ　54 ⒶⒷⒸⒹ

5 ⒶⒷⒸⒹ　15 ⒶⒷⒸⒹ　25 ⒶⒷⒸⒹ　35 ⒶⒷⒸⒹ　45 ⒶⒷⒸⒹ　55 ⒶⒷⒸⒹ

6 ⒶⒷⒸⒹ　16 ⒶⒷⒸⒹ　26 ⒶⒷⒸⒹ　36 ⒶⒷⒸⒹ　46 ⒶⒷⒸⒹ　56 ⒶⒷⒸⒹ

7 ⒶⒷⒸⒹ　17 ⒶⒷⒸⒹ　27 ⒶⒷⒸⒹ　37 ⒶⒷⒸⒹ　47 ⒶⒷⒸⒹ　57 ⒶⒷⒸⒹ

8 ⒶⒷⒸⒹ　18 ⒶⒷⒸⒹ　28 ⒶⒷⒸⒹ　38 ⒶⒷⒸⒹ　48 ⒶⒷⒸⒹ　58 ⒶⒷⒸⒹ

9 ⒶⒷⒸⒹ　19 ⒶⒷⒸⒹ　29 ⒶⒷⒸⒹ　39 ⒶⒷⒸⒹ　49 ⒶⒷⒸⒹ　59 ⒶⒷⒸⒹ

10 ⒶⒷⒸⒹ　20 ⒶⒷⒸⒹ　30 ⒶⒷⒸⒹ　40 ⒶⒷⒸⒹ　50 ⒶⒷⒸⒹ　60 ⒶⒷⒸⒹ

English Listening Comprehension Test

Test Book No. 12

This listening comprehension test will test your ability to understand spoken English. In this test, each conversation, statement and question will be spoken JUST ONE TIME. They will not be written out for you. There are four parts to this test. Special instructions will be given to you at the beginning of each part.

Part A

In Part A, you will see several pictures in your test book. For each picture, you will be asked 1 to 3 questions.   For each question, you will hear four possible answers. Choose the best answer according to what you see in the picture.

Example:

You will see:

You will hear: What is this?
        A. This is a table.
        B. This is a chair.
        C. This is a watch.
        D. This is a doll.

The best answer to the question "What is this?" is B: "This is a chair."   Therefore, you should choose answer B.

A. Questions 1-3

B. Questions 4-6

C. Questions 7-9

D. Questions 10-12

E. Questions 13-15

Part B

In Part B, you will hear 15 questions.   After you hear a question, read the four possible answers in your test book and decide which one is the best answer to the question you have heard.

Example:

<u>You will hear:</u>   What does your father do?

<u>You will read:</u>   A. He's 50 years old.
                        B. He's a teacher.
                        C. He's hungry.
                        D. He's in Los Angeles.

The best answer to the question "What does your father do?" is B: "He's a teacher." Therefore, you should choose answer B.

Please go to the next page. ⇨

16. A. To the park.
    B. In the office.
    C. Yes, they are walking home.
    D. On campus.

17. A. By bus.
    B. He didn't sleep.
    C. It is summer.
    D. I don't know.

18. A. It's very cold.
    B. It snowed a lot.
    C. It usually snows.
    D. It was quite hot.

19. A. How much does one cost?
    B. How many do you need?
    C. How do I spend my money?
    D. How much money do I have?

20. A. I have a new watch.
    B. You can go by taxi.
    C. About twenty minutes.
    D. What time is it?

21. A. It's time to go.
    B. I hope so!
    C. So did I.
    D. Come in, John.

22. A. I've thought about it.
    B. I've done many of them.
    C. No. Can you help me with it?
    D. Yes, I have done them.

23. A. I can't believe it.
    B. I can't wait.
    C. Did you hear that?
    D. Yes, I know.

24. A. It never stays right here.
    B. It's right across the street.
    C. It goes to the park.
    D. They stop to take a bus.

25. A. Can I help you?
    B. Bring me a towel, please.
    C. I'll do anything I can.
    D. How can you do that?

26. A. It takes time.
    B. Do you want something to eat?
    C. Be careful.
    D. I'll get one for you.

27. A. I am at school.
    B. I am going to school.
    C. I am a student.
    D. I am doing my homework.

28. A. Yes, I don't have anything to do
       this afternoon.
    B. Can you go with me?
    C. I don't know yet.
    D. I did a lot of work this afternoon.

29. A. Of course, I am.
    B. Of course, I do.
    C. Who is that man?
    D. Who said that?

30. A. No, I never did that before.
    B. No, I never saw one before.
    C. Yes, I never did.
    D. No, I sometimes did.

Part C

In Part C, you will hear 15 conversations between a man and a woman. After each conversation, you will hear a question about the conversation. After you hear the question, read the four possible answers in your test book and choose the best answer to the question you have heard.

Example:

You will hear:　(Man)　　How do you go to school every day?
　　　　　　　　(Woman)　Usually by bus.　Sometimes by taxi.

　　　　　　　　TONE:　　How does the woman go to school?

You will read:　A.　She always goes to school on foot.
　　　　　　　　B.　She usually takes a bike.
　　　　　　　　C.　She takes either a bus or a taxi.
　　　　　　　　D.　She usually goes to school by bus, never by taxi.

The best answer to the question "How does the woman go to school?" is C: "She takes either a bus or a taxi." Therefore, you should choose answer C.

Please go to the next page. ⇨

31. A. A visitor has borrowed it.
    B. She had given it to her guide.
    C. A friend took it to the West.
    D. Bill gave it back to his friend.

32. A. In a drugstore.
    B. In a hardware store.
    C. In a snack bar.
    D. In a bakery.

33. A. Picking up ice cubes.
    B. Betting all forty dollars.
    C. Leaving in forty minutes.
    D. Leaving immediately.

34. A. Feeling sorry for himself.
    B. Asking for change.
    C. Trying to purchase two pickles.
    D. Sending a package.

35. A. One.
    B. Two.
    C. Three.
    D. Six.

36. A. It has a lot of students in it.
    B. It's going to be a lot of fun.
    C. It's going to require a lot of reading.
    D. It seems to be working out quite well.

37. A. The new driveway has been completed.
    B. The store was damaged.
    C. The work wasn't properly done.
    D. The area is flooded after the rain.

38. A. She was unsure of how Jill really felt.
    B. She didn't like it.
    C. She was excited about it.
    D. She was sure she wouldn't use it.

39. A. Use the back door.
    B. Fail to deliver his package.
    C. See a different person.
    D. Act in front of an audience.

40. A. He surprised the woman during dinner.
    B. He went to exactly two shops.
    C. He bought something that wasn't on the list.
    D. He brought home someone she wasn't expecting.

41. A. Where to have her shoes fixed.
    B. What the latest scandal was.
    C. How to get to the other side of the intersection.
    D. Which section of town is best for shopping.

42. A. The director spoke too long.
    B. The actors were not very good.
    C. It was difficult to follow the action.
    D. There was too little action.

43. A. It's time for his eye drops.
    B. He should clean up what he dropped.
    C. He should pour more water in the glasses.
    D. It's perfectly clear outside.

44. A. Apply for the fellowship.
    B. Take a statistics course.
    C. Check her background research.
    D. Pick a more opportune moment.

45. A. They've been working at the telescope for two days.
    B. They can't find the microscope.
    C. They've been working in the laboratory for two hours.
    D. They can't fix the microphone.

Part D

In Part D, you will hear 15 short talks. After each talk, you will hear a question about the talk. After you hear the question, read the four possible answers in your test book and choose the best answer to the question you have heard.

Example:

You will hear:　Well, that's all for Unit 15. For today's homework, please do the review questions on page 80, and we'll check the answers tomorrow. Now, let's go on to Unit 16.

TONE: What is the teacher going to do next in today's class?

You will read:　A. Check the homework.
　　　　　　　　B. Review Unit 15.
　　　　　　　　C. Start a new unit.
　　　　　　　　D. Answer students' questions.

The best answer to the question "What is the teacher going to do next in today's class?" is C: "Start a new unit." Therefore, you should choose answer C.

Please go to the next page. ⇨

46. A. Take a cooking class.
    B. Have dinner at home.
    C. Go to Mexico.
    D. Go out to a Mexican restaurant.

47. A. Studied biographies.
    B. Kept busy.
    C. Visited his parents.
    D. Worked in a restaurant.

48. A. Tama is the cutest cat.
    B. Tama sleeps with her.
    C. Tama is the youngest cat.
    D. Tama wakes her up.

49. A. The front page.
    B. The sports page.
    C. The comics.
    D. The business section.

50. A. He works for a hotel.
    B. He works for a transport company.
    C. He works in reception.
    D. He's a telephone engineer.

51. A. Morning.
    B. Afternoon.
    C. Night.
    D. It's impossible to tell.

52. A. 11:00.
    B. A quarter to five.
    C. 11:45.
    D. At four or five.

53. A. People who use a credit card a lot.
    B. People who make many monthly payments by check.
    C. People who have a large amount of money.
    D. People who need to start saving.

54. A. It catches only target fish.
    B. It is smaller.
    C. It is indiscriminate in what it catches.
    D. It is used only in the Pacific Ocean.

55. A. From 9:00 a.m. to 8:00 p.m.
    B. From 9:00 a.m. to 9:00 p.m.
    C. From 9:00 a.m. to midnight.
    D. From noon to 9:00 p.m.

56. A. Today's meeting.
    B. Additional meetings.
    C. Future farm subsidies.
    D. Yesterday's agreement.

57. A. An examiner.
    B. A taxi driver.
    C. A school teacher.
    D. A banker.

58. A. In an airport.
    B. At a port.
    C. In a city office.
    D. At a train station.

59. A. A first-class train ride all the way across Europe.
    B. Only three days of train travel among major European capitals.
    C. A whole month's unlimited second-class train travel.
    D. A two-month uninterrupted trip by train.

60. A. They sometimes get anxious and depressed.
    B. They usually need to see a doctor to receive medication.
    C. They don't develop symptoms at first.
    D. They feel worse when they return to coffee drinking.

中級英語聽力檢定測驗答案紙

中文姓名 _____　　　測驗日期：民國 _____ 年 _____ 月 _____ 日

1. 准考證號碼	2. 出　　生			3. 國民身分證統一編號
	年 (民國)	月	日	

請依序將每個數字在下欄塗黑

※注意：本答案紙限用 #2 (HB) 黑色
鉛筆在「○」內塗黑、塗滿。

作答樣例：　正　確　　　錯　誤

聽　力　測　驗				
試題別				
試題冊號碼				

1 Ⓐ Ⓑ Ⓒ Ⓓ　　11 Ⓐ Ⓑ Ⓒ Ⓓ　　21 Ⓐ Ⓑ Ⓒ Ⓓ　　31 Ⓐ Ⓑ Ⓒ Ⓓ　　41 Ⓐ Ⓑ Ⓒ Ⓓ　　51 Ⓐ Ⓑ Ⓒ Ⓓ

2 Ⓐ Ⓑ Ⓒ Ⓓ　　12 Ⓐ Ⓑ Ⓒ Ⓓ　　22 Ⓐ Ⓑ Ⓒ Ⓓ　　32 Ⓐ Ⓑ Ⓒ Ⓓ　　42 Ⓐ Ⓑ Ⓒ Ⓓ　　52 Ⓐ Ⓑ Ⓒ Ⓓ

3 Ⓐ Ⓑ Ⓒ Ⓓ　　13 Ⓐ Ⓑ Ⓒ Ⓓ　　23 Ⓐ Ⓑ Ⓒ Ⓓ　　33 Ⓐ Ⓑ Ⓒ Ⓓ　　43 Ⓐ Ⓑ Ⓒ Ⓓ　　53 Ⓐ Ⓑ Ⓒ Ⓓ

4 Ⓐ Ⓑ Ⓒ Ⓓ　　14 Ⓐ Ⓑ Ⓒ Ⓓ　　24 Ⓐ Ⓑ Ⓒ Ⓓ　　34 Ⓐ Ⓑ Ⓒ Ⓓ　　44 Ⓐ Ⓑ Ⓒ Ⓓ　　54 Ⓐ Ⓑ Ⓒ Ⓓ

5 Ⓐ Ⓑ Ⓒ Ⓓ　　15 Ⓐ Ⓑ Ⓒ Ⓓ　　25 Ⓐ Ⓑ Ⓒ Ⓓ　　35 Ⓐ Ⓑ Ⓒ Ⓓ　　45 Ⓐ Ⓑ Ⓒ Ⓓ　　55 Ⓐ Ⓑ Ⓒ Ⓓ

6 Ⓐ Ⓑ Ⓒ Ⓓ　　16 Ⓐ Ⓑ Ⓒ Ⓓ　　26 Ⓐ Ⓑ Ⓒ Ⓓ　　36 Ⓐ Ⓑ Ⓒ Ⓓ　　46 Ⓐ Ⓑ Ⓒ Ⓓ　　56 Ⓐ Ⓑ Ⓒ Ⓓ

7 Ⓐ Ⓑ Ⓒ Ⓓ　　17 Ⓐ Ⓑ Ⓒ Ⓓ　　27 Ⓐ Ⓑ Ⓒ Ⓓ　　37 Ⓐ Ⓑ Ⓒ Ⓓ　　47 Ⓐ Ⓑ Ⓒ Ⓓ　　57 Ⓐ Ⓑ Ⓒ Ⓓ

8 Ⓐ Ⓑ Ⓒ Ⓓ　　18 Ⓐ Ⓑ Ⓒ Ⓓ　　28 Ⓐ Ⓑ Ⓒ Ⓓ　　38 Ⓐ Ⓑ Ⓒ Ⓓ　　48 Ⓐ Ⓑ Ⓒ Ⓓ　　58 Ⓐ Ⓑ Ⓒ Ⓓ

9 Ⓐ Ⓑ Ⓒ Ⓓ　　19 Ⓐ Ⓑ Ⓒ Ⓓ　　29 Ⓐ Ⓑ Ⓒ Ⓓ　　39 Ⓐ Ⓑ Ⓒ Ⓓ　　49 Ⓐ Ⓑ Ⓒ Ⓓ　　59 Ⓐ Ⓑ Ⓒ Ⓓ

10 Ⓐ Ⓑ Ⓒ Ⓓ　　20 Ⓐ Ⓑ Ⓒ Ⓓ　　30 Ⓐ Ⓑ Ⓒ Ⓓ　　40 Ⓐ Ⓑ Ⓒ Ⓓ　　50 Ⓐ Ⓑ Ⓒ Ⓓ　　60 Ⓐ Ⓑ Ⓒ Ⓓ

English Listening Comprehension Test

Test Book No. 13

This listening comprehension test will test your ability to understand spoken English.   In this test, each conversation, statement and question will be spoken JUST ONE TIME.   They will not be written out for you.   There are four parts to this test. Special instructions will be given to you at the beginning of each part.

Part A

In Part A, you will see several pictures in your test book.   For each picture, you will be asked 1 to 3 questions.   For each question, you will hear four possible answers. Choose the best answer according to what you see in the picture.

Example:

You will see:

You will hear: What is this?
   A. This is a table.
   B. This is a chair.
   C. This is a watch.
   D. This is a doll.

The best answer to the question "What is this?" is B: "This is a chair."   Therefore, you should choose answer B.

A. Questions 1-4

C. Questions 9-11

B. Questions 5-8

D. Questions 12-15

Part B

In Part B, you will hear 15 questions.   After you hear a question, read the four possible answers in your test book and decide which one is the best answer to the question you have heard.

Example:

<u>You will hear</u>:   What does your father do?

<u>You will read</u>:   A. He's 50 years old.
B. He's a teacher.
C. He's hungry.
D. He's in Los Angeles.

The best answer to the question "What does your father do?" is B: "He's a teacher." Therefore, you should choose answer B.

Please go to the next page. ⇨

16. A. How do you do?
    B. Good morning.
    C. See you later.
    D. How are you?

17. A. That's all right.
    B. No, I am not.
    C. Yes, he does.
    D. Yes, he is.

18. A. Helen didn't do it.
    B. Helen washed yesterday.
    C. Helen did.
    D. Helen did it this morning.

19. A. How nice is it!
    B. I bought something in that store yesterday.
    C. Is that store on sale?
    D. We can go there and buy some things we need.

20. A. He just caught a cold.
    B. Something will happen to her.
    C. She was sick.
    D. She is right.

21. A. Very soon.
    B. In five minutes.
    C. Every three minutes.
    D. About five minutes.

22. A. Because I'm going to have an English test.
    B. I became interested in all the subjects.
    C. I was bored with all the subjects.
    D. Because I got good grades in English.

23. A. Mary called up.
    B. Tom calls for me.
    C. It is Peter.
    D. I called Mary up.

24. A. Fine, thanks.
    B. Yes, I did.
    C. Yes, we have.
    D. Yes, I have.

25. A. I'll take a bus.
    B. I'll go in the morning.
    C. I'll walk there.
    D. I'll go to my friend's.

26. A. I bought it five hundred dollars.
    B. My sweater took me five hundred dollars.
    C. It costs too much.
    D. I spent three hundred dollars on it.

27. A. Not at all.
    B. O.K. That is a good idea.
    C. No, please.
    D. Yes, thanks.

28. A. Yes, I do.
    B. Yes, please.
    C. Please, I do.
    D. Yes, I do, please.

29. A. Ten minutes.
    B. It's a long way.
    C. It's five minutes slow.
    D. It isn't far.

30. A. He is a soldier.
    B. He is Mr. Green, my doctor.
    C. He is a tall man.
    D. He is very well.

Part C

In Part C, you will hear 15 conversations between a man and a woman.   After each conversation, you will hear a question about the conversation.   After you hear the question, read the four possible answers in your test book and choose the best answer to the question you have heard.

Example:

<u>You will hear</u>:   (Man)   How do you go to school every day?
(Woman)   Usually by bus.   Sometimes by taxi.

TONE: How does the woman go to school?

<u>You will read</u>:   A. She always goes to school on foot.
B. She usually takes a bike.
C. She takes either a bus or a taxi.
D. She usually goes to school by bus, never by taxi.

The best answer to the question "How does the woman go to school?" is C: "She takes either a bus or a taxi."   Therefore, you should choose answer C.

Please go to the next page. ⇨

31. A. The cablevision is not working.
　　B. All of them but channel seventeen.
　　C. Channel seventeen.
　　D. All of them.

32. A. Mr. Davis.
　　B. Mr. Davis' secretary.
　　C. Mr. Ward.
　　D. Mr. Thomas.

33. A. At a bank.
　　B. At a grocery store.
　　C. At a doctor's office.
　　D. At a gas station.

34. A. The man is too tired to go to the movie.
　　B. The woman wants to go to the movie.
　　C. The man wants to go out to dinner.
　　D. The woman does not want to go to the movie.

35. A. He will borrow some typing paper from the woman.
　　B. He will lend the woman some typing paper.
　　C. He will type the woman's paper.
　　D. He will buy some typing paper for the woman.

36. A. $60.
　　B. $100.
　　C. $120.
　　D. $200.

37. A. Two blocks.
　　B. Three blocks.
　　C. Four blocks.
　　D. Five blocks.

38. A. In a library.
　　B. In a hotel.
　　C. In a hospital.
　　D. In an elevator.

39. A. The man's father did not go.
　　B. The man thought that the game was excellent.
　　C. They thought that the game was unsatisfactory.
　　D. The man thought that the game was excellent, but his father thought that it was unsatisfactory.

40. A. $150.
　　B. $175.
　　C. $200.
　　D. $225.

41. A. Patient-Doctor.
　　B. Waitress-Customer.
　　C. Wife-Husband.
　　D. Secretary-Boss.

42. A. That the speakers did not go to the meeting.
　　B. That the woman went to the meeting, but the man did not.
　　C. That the man went to the meeting, but the woman did not.
　　D. That both speakers went to the meeting.

43. A. By December thirtieth.
　　B. By New Year's.
　　C. By December third.
　　D. By December thirteenth.

44. A. The operator.
　　B. The person receiving the call.
　　C. The person making the call.
　　D. No one.　The call is free.

45. A. At the bank.
　　B. At the market.
　　C. At the nursery.
　　D. At the hardware store.

Part D

In Part D, you will hear 15 short talks.   After each talk, you will hear a question about the talk.   After you hear the question, read the four possible answers in your test book and choose the best answer to the question you have heard.

Example:

<u>You will hear:</u>   Well, that's all for Unit 15.   For today's homework, please do the review questions on page 80, and we'll check the answers tomorrow. Now, let's go on to Unit 16.

TONE: What is the teacher going to do next in today's class?

<u>You will read:</u>   A. Check the homework.
B. Review Unit 15.
C. Start a new unit.
D. Answer students' questions.

The best answer to the question "What is the teacher going to do next in today's class?" is C: "Start a new unit."   Therefore, you should choose answer C.

Please go to the next page. ⇨

46. A. He goes swimming..
    B. He goes fishing.
    C. He takes a long walk.
    D. He works in the field.

47. A. He used a stove and burned wood.
    B. He lived on an island.
    C. He shopped on the mainland.
    D. He took a ferry.

48. A. He had been to the town before.
    B. He asked a policeman for help.
    C. His friends gave him a clear map.
    D. His map was difficult to understand.

49. A. She takes a bus.
    B. She takes a train.
    C. She takes an extra two hours.
    D. She plans to take a plane.

50. A. A computer engineer.
    B. A salesperson.
    C. A track athlete.
    D. A computer expert.

51. A. A dance.
    B. A barbecue.
    C. A cooking class.
    D. An outdoor theater production.

52. A. 10.00 seconds.
    B. 10.02 seconds.
    C. 10.22 seconds.
    D. 10.20 seconds.

53. A. Smoking at home.
    B. Smoking in all New York restaurants, regardless of size.
    C. Changing the regulations on smoking.
    D. Smoking in almost all public places in New York.

54. A. Food and oxygen.
    B. Food and water.
    C. Water and beauty.
    D. Diversity and proportion.

55. A. California's is about the same as Australia's.
    B. California's is about twenty times larger.
    C. California's is nearly two times larger.
    D. California's is about half of Australia's.

56. A. Gram.
    B. Vitamin B.
    C. Ascorbic acid.
    D. Health tip.

57. A. To make flour.
    B. To take the place of rice.
    C. To give food a different taste.
    D. To process a food.

58. A. A college professor.
    B. A book salesman.
    C. A librarian.
    D. A poet.

59. A. The whole of it.
    B. None of it.
    C. The east side.
    D. The west side.

60. A. The cafés served a wide variety of food.
    B. The cups of coffee were much larger.
    C. The customers had their favorite waiters.
    D. The customers could relax for hours over coffee.

中級英語聽力檢定測驗答案紙

中文姓名 _____　　　測驗日期：民國 _____ 年 _____ 月 _____ 日

1. 准考證號碼	2. 出　　　生			3. 國民身分證統一編號
請依序將每個數字在下欄塗黑	年(民國)	月	日	

請依序將每個數字在下欄塗黑

准考證號碼欄位數字：⓪①②③④⑤⑥⑦⑧⑨

出生年(民國)：⓪①②③④⑤⑥⑦⑧⑨
月：⓪①
日：⓪①②③

國民身分證統一編號：
Ⓐ Ⓑ Ⓒ Ⓓ Ⓔ Ⓕ Ⓖ Ⓗ Ⓘ Ⓙ Ⓚ Ⓛ Ⓜ Ⓝ Ⓞ Ⓟ Ⓠ Ⓡ Ⓢ Ⓣ Ⓤ Ⓥ Ⓦ Ⓧ Ⓨ Ⓩ
數字欄位：⓪①②③④⑤⑥⑦⑧⑨

＊注意：本答案紙限用 #2 (HB) 黑色
鉛筆在「〇」內塗黑、塗滿。

作答樣例：　正　確　　　錯　誤

正確：Ⓐ Ⓑ ● Ⓓ

錯誤：
Ⓐ Ⓑ ⊘ Ⓓ
Ⓐ Ⓑ ⊗ Ⓓ
Ⓐ Ⓑ ◉ Ⓓ
Ⓐ Ⓑ ◐ Ⓓ

聽　力　測　驗			
試題別			
試題冊號碼			

1 ⒶⒷⒸⒹ　11 ⒶⒷⒸⒹ　21 ⒶⒷⒸⒹ　31 ⒶⒷⒸⒹ　41 ⒶⒷⒸⒹ　51 ⒶⒷⒸⒹ

2 ⒶⒷⒸⒹ　12 ⒶⒷⒸⒹ　22 ⒶⒷⒸⒹ　32 ⒶⒷⒸⒹ　42 ⒶⒷⒸⒹ　52 ⒶⒷⒸⒹ

3 ⒶⒷⒸⒹ　13 ⒶⒷⒸⒹ　23 ⒶⒷⒸⒹ　33 ⒶⒷⒸⒹ　43 ⒶⒷⒸⒹ　53 ⒶⒷⒸⒹ

4 ⒶⒷⒸⒹ　14 ⒶⒷⒸⒹ　24 ⒶⒷⒸⒹ　34 ⒶⒷⒸⒹ　44 ⒶⒷⒸⒹ　54 ⒶⒷⒸⒹ

5 ⒶⒷⒸⒹ　15 ⒶⒷⒸⒹ　25 ⒶⒷⒸⒹ　35 ⒶⒷⒸⒹ　45 ⒶⒷⒸⒹ　55 ⒶⒷⒸⒹ

6 ⒶⒷⒸⒹ　16 ⒶⒷⒸⒹ　26 ⒶⒷⒸⒹ　36 ⒶⒷⒸⒹ　46 ⒶⒷⒸⒹ　56 ⒶⒷⒸⒹ

7 ⒶⒷⒸⒹ　17 ⒶⒷⒸⒹ　27 ⒶⒷⒸⒹ　37 ⒶⒷⒸⒹ　47 ⒶⒷⒸⒹ　57 ⒶⒷⒸⒹ

8 ⒶⒷⒸⒹ　18 ⒶⒷⒸⒹ　28 ⒶⒷⒸⒹ　38 ⒶⒷⒸⒹ　48 ⒶⒷⒸⒹ　58 ⒶⒷⒸⒹ

9 ⒶⒷⒸⒹ　19 ⒶⒷⒸⒹ　29 ⒶⒷⒸⒹ　39 ⒶⒷⒸⒹ　49 ⒶⒷⒸⒹ　59 ⒶⒷⒸⒹ

10 ⒶⒷⒸⒹ　20 ⒶⒷⒸⒹ　30 ⒶⒷⒸⒹ　40 ⒶⒷⒸⒹ　50 ⒶⒷⒸⒹ　60 ⒶⒷⒸⒹ

English Listening Comprehension Test

Test Book No. 14

This listening comprehension test will test your ability to understand spoken English.　In this test, each conversation, statement and question will be spoken JUST ONE TIME.　They will not be written out for you.　There are four parts to this test. Special instructions will be given to you at the beginning of each part.

Part A

In Part A, you will see several pictures in your test book.　For each picture, you will be asked 1 to 3 questions.　For each question, you will hear four possible answers. Choose the best answer according to what you see in the picture.

Example:

You will see:

You will hear:　What is this?
     A.　This is a table.
     B.　This is a chair.
     C.　This is a watch.
     D.　This is a doll.

The best answer to the question "What is this?" is B: "This is a chair."　Therefore, you should choose answer B.

A. <u>Questions 1-2</u>

D. <u>Questions 7-9</u>

B. <u>Questions 3-4</u>

E. <u>Questions 10-12</u>

C. <u>Questions 5-6</u>

F. <u>Questions 13-15</u>

Part B

In Part B, you will hear 15 questions. After you hear a question, read the four possible answers in your test book and decide which one is the best answer to the question you have heard.

Example:

<u>You will hear:</u>　What does your father do?

<u>You will read:</u>　A. He's 50 years old.
　　　　　　　　　B. He's a teacher.
　　　　　　　　　C. He's hungry.
　　　　　　　　　D. He's in Los Angeles.

The best answer to the question "What does your father do?" is B: "He's a teacher." Therefore, you should choose answer B.

Please go to the next page. ⇨

16. A. It's Saturday.
    B. It's cold.
    C. It's winter.
    D. It's ten o'clock.

17. A. Yes, please.
    B. Yes, but not much.
    C. Yes, many.
    D. Yes, we have a lot of.

18. A. Usually five days a week.
    B. She works only at night.
    C. She always works hard.
    D. Her work is quite easy.

19. A. He'll study English.
    B. Let's go to a movie.
    C. No, you are not going to do it.
    D. We played basketball.

20. A. That's a good idea.
    B. So do I.
    C. What's the problem?
    D. I hope so.

21. A. Good! But I have no time.
    B. Why not?
    C. What time is your flight?
    D. That's great.

22. A. She doesn't know it.
    B. Mine does, too.
    C. She must be home.
    D. Oh, doesn't she?

23. A. I'll do that, Mother.
    B. No, I don't.
    C. You are very kind to do so.
    D. No, thank you.

24. A. No, not today. Thank you.
    B. Thank you, sir.
    C. May I give you a hand?
    D. What do you need?

25. A. Excuse me. I want some.
    B. Not at all.
    C. Yes, please.
    D. Yes, I am.

26. A. The first scene has already started.
    B. No, I think it is your move, actually.
    C. I just started reading the book.
    D. I'm pleased to meet you.

27. A. Fine. Let's play ball.
    B. It certainly is.
    C. I need more time to decide.
    D. No, not yet.

28. A. Yes, it's not.
    B. No, I am not.
    C. Yes, they are.
    D. Yes, it is.

29. A. What is it about?
    B. Not at all. Thanks.
    C. Yes, we will.
    D. I'd love to.

30. A. I think those are my pens.
    B. I think it is my pen.
    C. I think that is my friend.
    D. I think those are my friends.

Part C

In Part C, you will hear 15 conversations between a man and a woman. After each conversation, you will hear a question about the conversation. After you hear the question, read the four possible answers in your test book and choose the best answer to the question you have heard.

Example:

You will hear: (Man) How do you go to school every day?
(Woman) Usually by bus. Sometimes by taxi.

TONE: How does the woman go to school?

You will read: A. She always goes to school on foot.
B. She usually takes a bike.
C. She takes either a bus or a taxi.
D. She usually goes to school by bus, never by taxi.

The best answer to the question "How does the woman go to school?" is C: "She takes either a bus or a taxi." Therefore, you should choose answer C.

Please go to the next page. ⟹

31. A. After five.
    B. At or before five.
    C. In the morning.
    D. Late at night.

32. A. Studying.
    B. Relaxing.
    C. Taking a test.
    D. Studying subjects other than math.

33. A. A few days.
    B. We don't know.
    C. A couple of weeks.
    D. Just one week.

34. A. It doesn't work.
    B. It only works temporarily.
    C. It's really effective.
    D. It has harmful side effects.

35. A. She hates it.
    B. It makes her mad.
    C. She is embarrassed.
    D. She likes it very much.

36. A. He isn't interested.
    B. He's scared.
    C. He doesn't understand it.
    D. He's mad at it.

37. A. She really likes the course.
    B. She wishes she hadn't taken it.
    C. She thinks the course is too late.
    D. She has no interest in it.

38. A. He can talk without preparing.
    B. He can speak standing up.
    C. He likes to talk without thinking.
    D. He talks with his toes.

39. A. He's too embarrassed.
    B. He has no interest in that movie.
    C. He's boo busy.
    D. He has no money.

40. A. A credit card.
    B. A driver's license.
    C. A magazine subscription.
    D. None of the above.

41. A. California.
    B. New York.
    C. The South.
    D. Michigan.

42. A. He's angry because he lost some clothing.
    B. He's angry because he lost his money.
    C. He's sad because he lost his job.
    D. He was scolded for not wearing a shirt.

43. A. Move.
    B. Get a puppy.
    C. Transfer.
    D. Buy a cat.

44. A. A car almost hit her.
    B. She shook someone.
    C. Someone shook her.
    D. Someone chased her.

45. A. Driving in a car.
    B. Watching a movie.
    C. Eating dinner.
    D. Dancing.

Part D

In Part D, you will hear 15 short talks.   After each talk, you will hear a question about the talk.   After you hear the question, read the four possible answers in your test book and choose the best answer to the question you have heard.

Example:

<u>You will hear:</u>   Well, that's all for Unit 15.   For today's homework, please do the review questions on page 80, and we'll check the answers tomorrow. Now, let's go on to Unit 16.

TONE: What is the teacher going to do next in today's class?

<u>You will read:</u>   A. Check the homework.
B. Review Unit 15.
C. Start a new unit.
D. Answer students' questions.

The best answer to the question "What is the teacher going to do next in today's class?" is C: "Start a new unit."   Therefore, you should choose answer C.

Please go to the next page. ⇨

46. A. To make many friends.
    B. To have a big family.
    C. So that everyone can sit together.
    D. So that everyone can eat dinner quickly.

47. A. So that there would be no misunderstanding.
    B. So that he could buy from a local store.
    C. So that he could speak with a clerk.
    D. So that the computer software could not be found.

48. A. They like watching movies twice.
    B. They missed the beginning of the movie.
    C. They didn't find the theater after all.
    D. They didn't like that movie very much.

49. A. For her long vacation.
    B. At 10:30 in the next morning.
    C. For a couple of hours.
    D. For about seven hours.

50. A. 6.
    B. 10.
    C. 13.
    D. 30.

51. A. At an airport.
    B. At a hospital.
    C. In a department store.
    D. At a school.

52. A. 40%.
    B. 14%.
    C. 20%.
    D. 26%.

53. A. Mountain climbing.
    B. Skiing.
    C. Car racing.
    D. Windsurfing.

54. A. In Long Beach.
    B. In Sandy Head.
    C. In Cape Hook.
    D. In Silver Cup.

55. A. One of the major highways was shut down.
    B. There have been many traffic accidents.
    C. A lot of the roads are being repaired.
    D. Due to rain, many roads are flooded.

56. A. He has been given an award.
    B. He is presenting an award.
    C. He is trying to raise money.
    D. He is trying to get support.

57. A. Several million years.
    B. 10 million years.
    C. 40 million years.
    D. Over 40 million years.

58. A. In the Far North.
    B. In Oakland.
    C. In San Francisco.
    D. In New York.

59. A. The weather equipment was destroyed by the storms.
    B. Heavy rain damaged the weather equipment.
    C. The weather equipment was not able to pick up developing tornadoes.
    D. Nobody could operate the new weather equipment properly.

60. A. Half the risk for nonsmokers.
    B. Double the risk for nonsmokers.
    C. Five and a half times the risk for nonsmokers.
    D. 85 percent of the risk for nonsmokers.

中級英語聽力檢定測驗答案紙

中文姓名 _____　　測驗日期：民國 ____ 年 ____ 月 ____ 日

1. 准考證號碼	2. 出　　生			3. 國民身分證統一編號
	年(民國)	月	日	

請依序將每個數字在下欄塗黑

准考證號碼欄位：
⓪①②③④⑤⑥⑦⑧⑨（每欄）

出生年(民國)：⓪①②③④⑤⑥⑦⑧⑨
月：⓪①②③④⑤⑥⑦⑧⑨
日：①（十位）⓪①②③④⑤⑥⑦⑧⑨

國民身分證統一編號：
(A)(B)(C)(D)(E)(F)(H)(I)(J)(K)(L)(M)(N)(O)(P)(Q)(R)(S)(T)(U)(V)(W)(X)(Y)(Z)
⓪①②③④⑤⑥⑦⑧⑨（各數字欄）

*注意：本答案紙限用 #2 (HB) 黑色鉛筆在「○」內塗黑、塗滿。

作答樣例：　正　確　　　錯　誤
正確：(A)(B)●(D)
錯誤：(A)(B)✓(D)　(A)(B)✗(D)　(A)(B)(C)◯(D)　(A)(B)◖(D)

聽　力　測　驗				
試題別				
試題冊號碼				

1 (A)(B)(C)(D)　　11 (A)(B)(C)(D)　　21 (A)(B)(C)(D)　　31 (A)(B)(C)(D)　　41 (A)(B)(C)(D)　　51 (A)(B)(C)(D)
2 (A)(B)(C)(D)　　12 (A)(B)(C)(D)　　22 (A)(B)(C)(D)　　32 (A)(B)(C)(D)　　42 (A)(B)(C)(D)　　52 (A)(B)(C)(D)
3 (A)(B)(C)(D)　　13 (A)(B)(C)(D)　　23 (A)(B)(C)(D)　　33 (A)(B)(C)(D)　　43 (A)(B)(C)(D)　　53 (A)(B)(C)(D)
4 (A)(B)(C)(D)　　14 (A)(B)(C)(D)　　24 (A)(B)(C)(D)　　34 (A)(B)(C)(D)　　44 (A)(B)(C)(D)　　54 (A)(B)(C)(D)
5 (A)(B)(C)(D)　　15 (A)(B)(C)(D)　　25 (A)(B)(C)(D)　　35 (A)(B)(C)(D)　　45 (A)(B)(C)(D)　　55 (A)(B)(C)(D)
6 (A)(B)(C)(D)　　16 (A)(B)(C)(D)　　26 (A)(B)(C)(D)　　36 (A)(B)(C)(D)　　46 (A)(B)(C)(D)　　56 (A)(B)(C)(D)
7 (A)(B)(C)(D)　　17 (A)(B)(C)(D)　　27 (A)(B)(C)(D)　　37 (A)(B)(C)(D)　　47 (A)(B)(C)(D)　　57 (A)(B)(C)(D)
8 (A)(B)(C)(D)　　18 (A)(B)(C)(D)　　28 (A)(B)(C)(D)　　38 (A)(B)(C)(D)　　48 (A)(B)(C)(D)　　58 (A)(B)(C)(D)
9 (A)(B)(C)(D)　　19 (A)(B)(C)(D)　　29 (A)(B)(C)(D)　　39 (A)(B)(C)(D)　　49 (A)(B)(C)(D)　　59 (A)(B)(C)(D)
10 (A)(B)(C)(D)　　20 (A)(B)(C)(D)　　30 (A)(B)(C)(D)　　40 (A)(B)(C)(D)　　50 (A)(B)(C)(D)　　60 (A)(B)(C)(D)

English Listening Comprehension Test

Test Book No. 15

This listening comprehension test will test your ability to understand spoken English. In this test, each conversation, statement and question will be spoken JUST ONE TIME. They will not be written out for you. There are four parts to this test. Special instructions will be given to you at the beginning of each part.

Part A

In Part A, you will see several pictures in your test book. For each picture, you will be asked 1 to 3 questions. For each question, you will hear four possible answers. Choose the best answer according to what you see in the picture.

Example:

You will see:

You will hear: What is this?
A. This is a table.
B. This is a chair.
C. This is a watch.
D. This is a doll.

The best answer to the question "What is this?" is B: "This is a chair."   Therefore, you should choose answer B.

A. Questions 1-4

B. Questions 5-7

C. Questions 8-10

D. Questions 11-13

E. Questions 14-15

Part B

In Part B, you will hear 15 questions.   After you hear a question, read the four possible answers in your test book and decide which one is the best answer to the question you have heard.

Example:

<u>You will hear</u>:   What does your father do?

<u>You will read</u>:   A. He's 50 years old.
                           B. He's a teacher.
                           C. He's hungry.
                           D. He's in Los Angeles.

The best answer to the question "What does your father do?" is B: "He's a teacher." Therefore, you should choose answer B.

Please go to the next page. ⇨

16. A. No, you weren't.
    B. Yes, you were.
    C. Yes, I was.
    D. No, I was.

17. A. Sure, I don't.
    B. No, she speaks too fast.
    C. Yes, please.
    D. All right.

18. A. Yes, I'd like to.
    B. Yes, I like it.
    C. No, I wouldn't like.
    D. Do you have enough time?

19. A. Yes, a medium cola, please.
    B. Yes, you are boring.
    C. Yes, these are on sale.
    D. Yes, I want to.

20. A. Much better, thanks.
    B. I feel you're right.
    C. I don't feel like taking a walk now.
    D. This cloth feels soft.

21. A. For two o'clock.
    B. For two hours.
    C. Yes, I have watched it.
    D. About one o'clock.

22. A. The one without chemicals is.
    B. I know. Ants hate clean places.
    C. We changed our minds.
    D. How's everything?

23. A. If I knew, I would tell you where she lives.
    B. She had told me where she lives two days ago.
    C. If I were you, I would be angry.
    D. If I had told you where she lives, she would be angry.

24. A. It really doesn't matter.
    B. Yes, thank you.
    C. Yes, I'd like to buy these things.
    D. I'm sorry. This jelly is too old.

25. A. I have only one truck.
    B. I will give you five.
    C. The more, the better.
    D. I need a lot of time.

26. A. I know milk shakes will make you tired.
    B. I know milk shakes will make you fat.
    C. I know milk shakes will make you hungry.
    D. I know milk shakes will make you wait.

27. A. So has mine.
    B. Mine does, too.
    C. But mine hasn't.
    D. Mine doesn't, either.

28. A. He's on English lesson.
    B. He's not studying lesson nine.
    C. He's on Lesson Ten.
    D. Lesson Eight is quite easy.

29. A. No, I told you nothing.
    B. No, no.
    C. Thank you, too.
    D. You are welcome.

30. A. Yes, I have a new computer.
    B. Yes, I'd like to buy one.
    C. Yes, I'll use it tomorrow.
    D. Yes, it helps a lot.

Part C

In Part C, you will hear 15 conversations between a man and a woman. After each conversation, you will hear a question about the conversation. After you hear the question, read the four possible answers in your test book and choose the best answer to the question you have heard.

Example:

You will hear:　(Man)　　How do you go to school every day?
　　　　　　　　(Woman)　Usually by bus. Sometimes by taxi.

　　　　　　　　TONE:　　How does the woman go to school?

You will read:　A. She always goes to school on foot.
　　　　　　　　B. She usually takes a bike.
　　　　　　　　C. She takes either a bus or a taxi.
　　　　　　　　D. She usually goes to school by bus, never by taxi.

The best answer to the question "How does the woman go to school?" is C: "She takes either a bus or a taxi." Therefore, you should choose answer C.

Please go to the next page. ⇨

31. A. She is pleased to know about their moving.
    B. Moving to the east is better than to the west.
    C. Probably she will be content.
    D. She is a little disappointed.

32. A. The man got the flu.
    B. The woman went to school.
    C. Many students caught the flu.
    D. The junior high school was over earlier than usual.

33. A. Be ready for a panel discussion.
    B. Choose a topic and write a research paper.
    C. Read an assignment for two hours.
    D. Read chapters and summarize them.

34. A. Jim always plays at about the same level.
    B. Jim is very defensive.
    C. Jim plays a fair game.
    D. Jim's game is artificial.

35. A. That he's prepared for it.
    B. That it will be difficult.
    C. That he missed it.
    D. That it's hopeless to study for it.

36. A. Deliver the freezer.
    B. Defrost the meat.
    C. Obey the law.
    D. Freeze the meat.

37. A. She had already seen it.
    B. Her cousin paid her a visit.
    C. Her cousin stopped to buy something.
    D. Her watch stopped and she didn't know the time.

38. A. Apologetic.
    B. Angry.
    C. Annoyed.
    D. Disappointed.

39. A. He prefers his old set of clubs.
    B. He has little chance to play golf.
    C. He's playing better golf recently.
    D. He's too old to play much golf.

40. A. On a farm.
    B. In a slaughterhouse.
    C. In a market.
    D. In a convenience store.

41. A. In a taxi.
    B. On a bus.
    C. In an elevator.
    D. On a train.

42. A. In a hospital.
    B. In a beauty parlor.
    C. In a classroom.
    D. In a hotel room.

43. A. He is worried because he left his key.
    B. He took the wrong train.
    C. He lost his bike.
    D. He arrived at the office late.

44. A. She doesn't like funny horror movies.
    B. She's met a movie star recently.
    C. She would take action right away.
    D. She saw a comedian last Sunday.

45. A. 12 years.
    B. 11 years.
    C. A few days.
    D. A couple of weeks.

Part D

In Part D, you will hear 15 short talks. After each talk, you will hear a question about the talk. After you hear the question, read the four possible answers in your test book and choose the best answer to the question you have heard.

Example:

<u>You will hear:</u>   Well, that's all for Unit 15. For today's homework, please do the review questions on page 80, and we'll check the answers tomorrow. Now, let's go on to Unit 16.

TONE: What is the teacher going to do next in today's class?

<u>You will read:</u>   A. Check the homework.
B. Review Unit 15.
C. Start a new unit.
D. Answer students' questions.

The best answer to the question "What is the teacher going to do next in today's class?" is C: "Start a new unit." Therefore, you should choose answer C.

Please go to the next page. ⇨

46. A. To keep the weather very hot.
    B. To use less water.
    C. To use large amounts of water.
    D. To be very careful about the weather.

47. A. To rent a van.
    B. To go to a campground.
    C. To break down.
    D. To continue their vacation.

48. A. It has mild weather, good food, and jobs.
    B. There is plenty of work for farmers.
    C. Many airlines fly to and from this city.
    D. Frequent rain means lots of drinking water.

49. A. Big and quiet.
    B. Next to the station.
    C. Convenient but noisy.
    D. Not so convenient as the old one.

50. A. One a day.
    B. Two a day.
    C. One every other day.
    D. One a week.

51. A. Around the beginning of the century.
    B. In the 1920s.
    C. In the 1950s.
    D. This information is not given in the announcement.

52. A. Use public transportation.
    B. Take the Dock Street exit.
    C. Not use Franklin Pike or Madison Blvd.
    D. Not use the expressway.

53. A. Panicked.
    B. Left the ERM.
    C. Stabilized their currencies.
    D. Unified their markets.

54. A. Partly cloudy with a high of 60.
    B. Sunny with a high around 76.
    C. A 60 percent chance of rain.
    D. Rain with a high of 60.

55. A. 1:40 a.m.
    B. 8 p.m.
    C. 8 a.m.
    D. 9 p.m.

56. A. Five for a dollar.
    B. Twenty-nine cents a pound.
    C. Fifty-nine cents a pound.
    D. The speaker doesn't say.

57. A. They exercised a lot.
    B. They pulled many chariots.
    C. Through evolution.
    D. Men helped them to strengthen their legs.

58. A. In 1835.
    B. In 1935.
    C. In 1875.
    D. In 1895.

59. A. The trains arrived several hours late.
    B. Taxi drivers staged a demonstration.
    C. There was a serious traffic accident.
    D. Railway workers went on strike.

60. A. 5%.
    B. 10%.
    C. 25%.
    D. 50%.

中級英語聽力檢定測驗答案紙

中文姓名 _____   測驗日期：民國 ____ 年 ____ 月 ____ 日

1. 准考證號碼					2. 出 生						3. 國民身分證統一編號								
					年 (民國)		月	日												
請依序將每個數字在下欄塗黑																				

*注意：本答案紙限用 #2 (HB) 黑色
鉛筆在「○」內塗黑、塗滿。

作答樣例：　正　確　　　　錯　誤

Ⓐ Ⓑ ● Ⓓ

Ⓐ Ⓑ ☑ Ⓓ
Ⓐ Ⓑ ☒ Ⓓ
Ⓐ Ⓑ ◉ Ⓓ
Ⓐ Ⓑ ◗ Ⓓ

聽　力　測　驗				
試題別				
試題冊號碼				

1 Ⓐ Ⓑ Ⓒ Ⓓ	11 Ⓐ Ⓑ Ⓒ Ⓓ	21 Ⓐ Ⓑ Ⓒ Ⓓ	31 Ⓐ Ⓑ Ⓒ Ⓓ	41 Ⓐ Ⓑ Ⓒ Ⓓ	51 Ⓐ Ⓑ Ⓒ Ⓓ
2 Ⓐ Ⓑ Ⓒ Ⓓ	12 Ⓐ Ⓑ Ⓒ Ⓓ	22 Ⓐ Ⓑ Ⓒ Ⓓ	32 Ⓐ Ⓑ Ⓒ Ⓓ	42 Ⓐ Ⓑ Ⓒ Ⓓ	52 Ⓐ Ⓑ Ⓒ Ⓓ
3 Ⓐ Ⓑ Ⓒ Ⓓ	13 Ⓐ Ⓑ Ⓒ Ⓓ	23 Ⓐ Ⓑ Ⓒ Ⓓ	33 Ⓐ Ⓑ Ⓒ Ⓓ	43 Ⓐ Ⓑ Ⓒ Ⓓ	53 Ⓐ Ⓑ Ⓒ Ⓓ
4 Ⓐ Ⓑ Ⓒ Ⓓ	14 Ⓐ Ⓑ Ⓒ Ⓓ	24 Ⓐ Ⓑ Ⓒ Ⓓ	34 Ⓐ Ⓑ Ⓒ Ⓓ	44 Ⓐ Ⓑ Ⓒ Ⓓ	54 Ⓐ Ⓑ Ⓒ Ⓓ
5 Ⓐ Ⓑ Ⓒ Ⓓ	15 Ⓐ Ⓑ Ⓒ Ⓓ	25 Ⓐ Ⓑ Ⓒ Ⓓ	35 Ⓐ Ⓑ Ⓒ Ⓓ	45 Ⓐ Ⓑ Ⓒ Ⓓ	55 Ⓐ Ⓑ Ⓒ Ⓓ
6 Ⓐ Ⓑ Ⓒ Ⓓ	16 Ⓐ Ⓑ Ⓒ Ⓓ	26 Ⓐ Ⓑ Ⓒ Ⓓ	36 Ⓐ Ⓑ Ⓒ Ⓓ	46 Ⓐ Ⓑ Ⓒ Ⓓ	56 Ⓐ Ⓑ Ⓒ Ⓓ
7 Ⓐ Ⓑ Ⓒ Ⓓ	17 Ⓐ Ⓑ Ⓒ Ⓓ	27 Ⓐ Ⓑ Ⓒ Ⓓ	37 Ⓐ Ⓑ Ⓒ Ⓓ	47 Ⓐ Ⓑ Ⓒ Ⓓ	57 Ⓐ Ⓑ Ⓒ Ⓓ
8 Ⓐ Ⓑ Ⓒ Ⓓ	18 Ⓐ Ⓑ Ⓒ Ⓓ	28 Ⓐ Ⓑ Ⓒ Ⓓ	38 Ⓐ Ⓑ Ⓒ Ⓓ	48 Ⓐ Ⓑ Ⓒ Ⓓ	58 Ⓐ Ⓑ Ⓒ Ⓓ
9 Ⓐ Ⓑ Ⓒ Ⓓ	19 Ⓐ Ⓑ Ⓒ Ⓓ	29 Ⓐ Ⓑ Ⓒ Ⓓ	39 Ⓐ Ⓑ Ⓒ Ⓓ	49 Ⓐ Ⓑ Ⓒ Ⓓ	59 Ⓐ Ⓑ Ⓒ Ⓓ
10 Ⓐ Ⓑ Ⓒ Ⓓ	20 Ⓐ Ⓑ Ⓒ Ⓓ	30 Ⓐ Ⓑ Ⓒ Ⓓ	40 Ⓐ Ⓑ Ⓒ Ⓓ	50 Ⓐ Ⓑ Ⓒ Ⓓ	60 Ⓐ Ⓑ Ⓒ Ⓓ

English Listening Comprehension Test

Test Book No. 16

This listening comprehension test will test your ability to understand spoken English. In this test, each conversation, statement and question will be spoken JUST ONE TIME. They will not be written out for you. There are four parts to this test. Special instructions will be given to you at the beginning of each part.

Part A

In Part A, you will see several pictures in your test book. For each picture, you will be asked 1 to 3 questions. For each question, you will hear four possible answers. Choose the best answer according to what you see in the picture.

Example:

You will see:

You will hear: What is this?
A. This is a table.
B. This is a chair.
C. This is a watch.
D. This is a doll.

The best answer to the question "What is this?" is B: "This is a chair."   Therefore, you should choose answer B.

A. Questions 1-3

D. Questions 10-11

B. Questions 4-6

E. Questions 12-13

C. Questions 7-9

F. Questions 14-15

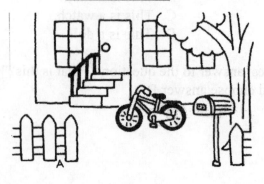

Part B

In Part B, you will hear 15 questions.   After you hear a question, read the four possible answers in your test book and decide which one is the best answer to the question you have heard.

Example:

<u>You will hear:</u>   What does your father do?

<u>You will read:</u>   A. He's 50 years old.
B. He's a teacher.
C. He's hungry.
D. He's in Los Angeles.

The best answer to the question "What does your father do?" is B: "He's a teacher." Therefore, you should choose answer B.

Please go to the next page. ⟹

16. A. No, they are not interested.
    B. No, it is boring.
    C. Yes, it is interested.
    D. Yes, it is boring.

17. A. Yes, he is.
    B. Yes, it is.
    C. He is.
    D. No, he is.

18. A. Yes, I can speak neither.
    B. No, I can't speak neither of them.
    C. I can speak both of them.
    D. Either of them will do.

19. A. Sure.
    B. I don't like it very much.
    C. No, I don't.
    D. Yes, I like it very much.

20. A. Oh, it's nothing.
    B. Any time.
    C. I don't mind at all.
    D. Not bad.

21. A. Please do.
    B. Here you are.
    C. There it is.
    D. Here it is.

22. A. February 8, 1999.
    B. 9:22.
    C. Monday.
    D. Tomorrow morning.

23. A. By bus.
    B. For fun.
    C. The smaller one.
    D. A teacher.

24. A. It's not Jack, I am sure.
    B. It is my friend Tom that will come to see us.
    C. Jane likes to knock at someone's door.
    D. It must be Sue.

25. A. How nice it is! Will you come with us?
    B. We will have that for nothing.
    C. You look great.
    D. We will pay for that.

26. A. It is $3.00 every.
    B. They are sold out.
    C. They are $3.00 each.   Children can get in at half price.
    D. The tickets are on the desk.

27. A. Twice a week.
    B. For two days.
    C. Last week.
    D. In my office.

28. A. What did you want?
    B. I'm sorry you didn't like it.
    C. I am glad you like it.
    D. Was it a present?

29. A. That's all right.
    B. Yes, she's very well.
    C. It's all right.
    D. Yes, she's very ill.

30. A. By bus.
    B. I am a stranger here.
    C. From China.
    D. An American.

Part C

In Part C, you will hear 15 conversations between a man and a woman. After each conversation, you will hear a question about the conversation. After you hear the question, read the four possible answers in your test book and choose the best answer to the question you have heard.

Example:

You will hear: (Man)   How do you go to school every day?
                 (Woman)   Usually by bus.   Sometimes by taxi.

                 TONE: How does the woman go to school?

You will read: A. She always goes to school on foot.
                 B. She usually takes a bike.
                 C. She takes either a bus or a taxi.
                 D. She usually goes to school by bus, never by taxi.

The best answer to the question "How does the woman go to school?" is C: "She takes either a bus or a taxi." Therefore, you should choose answer C.

Please go to the next page. ⇨

31. A. She agrees with the man.
    B. She doesn't know the book.
    C. She likes the book very much.
    D. She doesn't know what to do.

32. A. She can go with him this afternoon.
    B. She has a lot to do today.
    C. She's almost as busy as he is.
    D. She might be finished by noon.

33. A. The man should buy a different meal ticket each month.
    B. Individuals eat different amounts.
    C. Buying the meal ticket won't save the man money.
    D. The price of a meal varies from month to month.

34. A. Run in town.
    B. Look more carefully.
    C. Buying shoes from a catalogue.
    D. Find an easier place to exercise.

35. A. She doesn't like the professor very much.
    B. She doubts class will be canceled.
    C. She doesn't want to attend the conference.
    D. She wonders whether the professor is an accountant.

36. A. He doesn't expect to meet her at the seashore.
    B. He wants to know when she's coming.
    C. He wants to see how her experiment is progressing.
    D. He isn't interested in watching her.

37. A. Dan received them.
    B. Gloria forgot about them.
    C. Dan mailed them.
    D. Gloria has sent for them.

38. A. He's taller than anyone on campus.
    B. He's the best actor in the school.
    C. He's almost through with the campus tour.
    D. He's studying at college to be an actor.

39. A. She may need to take another course.
    B. The math course is too short.
    C. The graduation date has been changed.
    D. She should have gotten a better score.

40. A. Tea is better than coffee.
    B. The man should switch to tea.
    C. There are two reasons not to drink coffee.
    D. The man shouldn't drink either.

41. A. Accounting.
    B. Secretary.
    C. Sales.
    D. Guard.

42. A. An office worker.
    B. A police officer.
    C. A fellow passenger.
    D. A bell-hop.

43. A. For research.
    B. For pleasure.
    C. To see his family.
    D. For business.

44. A. Every week.
    B. Every month.
    C. Twice a month.
    D. Every other month.

45. A. Tom should quit smoking.
    B. Tom should buy cigarettes.
    C. Tom himself should think about where he smokes.
    D. Tom should go outside.

Part D

In Part D, you will hear 15 short talks.   After each talk, you will hear a question about the talk.   After you hear the question, read the four possible answers in your test book and choose the best answer to the question you have heard.

Example:

<u>You will hear:</u>   Well, that's all for Unit 15.   For today's homework, please do the review questions on page 80, and we'll check the answers tomorrow. Now, let's go on to Unit 16.

TONE: What is the teacher going to do next in today's class?

<u>You will read:</u>   A. Check the homework.
B. Review Unit 15.
C. Start a new unit.
D. Answer students' questions.

The best answer to the question "What is the teacher going to do next in today's class?" is C: "Start a new unit."   Therefore, you should choose answer C.

Please go to the next page. ⇨

46. A. He forgot to take pictures.
    B. He left it on the airplane.
    C. He bought it in Hawaii.
    D. Someone found it and sent it to him.

47. A. She damaged it slightly.
    B. She began driving it.
    C. She parked it at the supermarket.
    D. She damaged it seriously.

48. A. An hour early.
    B. To meet Jane.
    C. On Saturday.
    D. After her hiking trip with Jane.

49. A. On a train.
    B. On a plane.
    C. At a station.
    D. At Norfolk.

50. A. 1.1% less.
    B. 36% more.
    C. $86.4 billion more.
    D. 14.3% more.

51. A. Two days ago.
    B. Yesterday.
    C. This morning.
    D. This afternoon.

52. A. 277-9967.
    B. 276-2277.
    C. 277-7996.
    D. 279-7996.

53. A. At a university.
    B. At a high school.
    C. At a large corporation.
    D. In a government department.

54. A. Fifteen.
    B. Twenty-five.
    C. Fifty.
    D. Seventy-five.

55. A. Computers.
    B. Furniture.
    C. Lunch.
    D. Carpeting.

56. A. A movie that will be on television this weekend.
    B. A movie that starts showing soon at the theaters.
    C. A movie that has just come out on video.
    D. A movie that will be coming out on video soon.

57. A. Indonesia.
    B. Jakarta City.
    C. Batavia.
    D. Dutch East India.

58. A. It is usually cold in summer.
    B. It is usually warm in summer.
    C. It is both wet and cold in summer.
    D. It is rarely cold in summer.

59. A. Cigarette advertising.
    B. Government policies.
    C. Price increases for tobacco.
    D. Smoking-related diseases.

60. A. Cut the egg with a knife after cooking it.
    B. Turn the egg over while cooking it.
    C. Break the egg and poke the yolk before cooking it.
    D. Don't put the egg in a dish before cooking it.

中級英語聽力檢定測驗答案紙

中文姓名 _____　　測驗日期：民國 ____ 年 ____ 月 ____ 日

1. 准考證號碼	2. 出　　生			3. 國民身分證統一編號
請依序將每個數字在下欄塗黑	年(民國)	月	日	

（准考證號碼、出生、國民身分證統一編號塗黑欄：數字 0~9，身分證欄首列為英文字母 A~Z）

＊注意：本答案紙限用 #2 (HB) 黑色
　　　　鉛筆在「○」內塗黑、塗滿。

作答樣例：　正　確　　　錯　誤

正確：Ⓐ Ⓑ ● Ⓓ

錯誤：
Ⓐ Ⓑ ✓ Ⓓ
Ⓐ Ⓑ ✗ Ⓓ
Ⓐ Ⓑ ◐ Ⓓ
Ⓐ Ⓑ ⬤ Ⓓ

聽　力　測　驗			
試題別			
試題冊號碼			

1 ⒶⒷⒸⒹ　　11 ⒶⒷⒸⒹ　　21 ⒶⒷⒸⒹ　　31 ⒶⒷⒸⒹ　　41 ⒶⒷⒸⒹ　　51 ⒶⒷⒸⒹ
2 ⒶⒷⒸⒹ　　12 ⒶⒷⒸⒹ　　22 ⒶⒷⒸⒹ　　32 ⒶⒷⒸⒹ　　42 ⒶⒷⒸⒹ　　52 ⒶⒷⒸⒹ
3 ⒶⒷⒸⒹ　　13 ⒶⒷⒸⒹ　　23 ⒶⒷⒸⒹ　　33 ⒶⒷⒸⒹ　　43 ⒶⒷⒸⒹ　　53 ⒶⒷⒸⒹ
4 ⒶⒷⒸⒹ　　14 ⒶⒷⒸⒹ　　24 ⒶⒷⒸⒹ　　34 ⒶⒷⒸⒹ　　44 ⒶⒷⒸⒹ　　54 ⒶⒷⒸⒹ
5 ⒶⒷⒸⒹ　　15 ⒶⒷⒸⒹ　　25 ⒶⒷⒸⒹ　　35 ⒶⒷⒸⒹ　　45 ⒶⒷⒸⒹ　　55 ⒶⒷⒸⒹ
6 ⒶⒷⒸⒹ　　16 ⒶⒷⒸⒹ　　26 ⒶⒷⒸⒹ　　36 ⒶⒷⒸⒹ　　46 ⒶⒷⒸⒹ　　56 ⒶⒷⒸⒹ
7 ⒶⒷⒸⒹ　　17 ⒶⒷⒸⒹ　　27 ⒶⒷⒸⒹ　　37 ⒶⒷⒸⒹ　　47 ⒶⒷⒸⒹ　　57 ⒶⒷⒸⒹ
8 ⒶⒷⒸⒹ　　18 ⒶⒷⒸⒹ　　28 ⒶⒷⒸⒹ　　38 ⒶⒷⒸⒹ　　48 ⒶⒷⒸⒹ　　58 ⒶⒷⒸⒹ
9 ⒶⒷⒸⒹ　　19 ⒶⒷⒸⒹ　　29 ⒶⒷⒸⒹ　　39 ⒶⒷⒸⒹ　　49 ⒶⒷⒸⒹ　　59 ⒶⒷⒸⒹ
10 ⒶⒷⒸⒹ　　20 ⒶⒷⒸⒹ　　30 ⒶⒷⒸⒹ　　40 ⒶⒷⒸⒹ　　50 ⒶⒷⒸⒹ　　60 ⒶⒷⒸⒹ

心得筆記欄

中醫食療的智慧（養生藥膳篇）

編　著

2008年 11月 1日 第一版第一刷

ISBN 957-xxxx-xx-x

||||||||||||||| ● 學習出版公司門市部 ● |||||||||||||||||

台北地區：台北市許昌街 10 號 2 樓 TEL：(02)2331-4060・2331-9209
台中地區：台中市綠川東街 32 號 8 樓 23 室
　　　　　TEL：(04)223-2838

|||||||||||||||||||||||||||||||||||||||||||||||||||||||

中級英語聽力檢定②（教學專用本）

主　　　編／劉　毅
發　行　所／學習出版有限公司　　　　　☎ (02) 2704-5525
郵 撥 帳 號／0512727-2 學習出版社帳戶
登　記　證／局版台業 2179 號
印　刷　所／裕強彩色印刷有限公司
台 北 門 市／台北市許昌街 10 號 2 F　　　☎ (02) 2331-4060・2331-9209
台 中 門 市／台中市綠川東街 32 號 8 F 23 室　☎ (04) 223-2838
台灣總經銷／紅螞蟻圖書有限公司　　　　☎ (02) 2799-9490・2657-0132
美國總經銷／Evergreen Book Store　　　☎ (818) 2813622

售價：新台幣一百二十元正
2000 年 11 月 1 日一版二刷

ISBN 957-519-533-7